R0200715613

12/2019

P9-APG-872

PALM BEACH COUNTY
LIBRARY SYSTEM
3650 Summit Boulevard
West Palm Beach, FL 33406-4198

# SCOOBY-DOO! AND THE KARATE CAPER

Written by
James Gelsey

A
**LITTLE APPLE**
PAPERBACK

SCHOLASTIC INC.

New York   Toronto   London   Auckland   Sydney
Mexico City   New Delhi   Hong Kong   Buenos Aires

**visit us at www.abdopublishing.com**

Reinforced library bound edition published in 2011 by Spotlight, a division of the
ABDO Group, 8000 West 78th Street, Edina, Minnesota 55439. Spotlight produces
high-quality reinforced library bound editions for schools and libraries.
Published by agreement with Warner Bros.—A Time Warner Company.
All rights reserved. Used under authorization.

Printed in the United States of America, Melrose Park, Illinois.
052011
092011

 This book contains at least 10% recycled materials.

For Eden.

 Copyright © 2011 by Hanna-Barbera. SCOOBY-DOO and all related
characters and elements are trademarks of and © Hanna-Barbera.
WB SHIELD: ™ & © Warner Bros. Entertainment Inc.
(s11)

**Library of Congress Cataloging-in-Publication Data**
This title was previously cataloged with the following information:
Gelsey, James.
 Scooby-Doo! and the karate caper / written by James Gelsey
 -- Reinforced library bound ed.
 p. cm. -- (Scooby-Doo mysteries)
Summary: Scooby and Shaggy can't believe it when they hear their favorite restaurant, Louie's
Pizza Parlor, is about to close down. It turns out a creepy karate creature has been scaring away
all of Louie's customers. Now, for once in their lives, Scooby and Shaggy are determined to get to
the bottom of a mystery. After all, nothing better get between the two chums and their pizza!
1. Pizza--Fiction. 2. Restaurants--Fiction. 3.Karate--Fiction. 4. Dogs--Fiction.
5. Commercial buildings--Fiction. 6. Mystery and detective stories.
 PZ7.G2845 Sbn 2002
 [Fic]--dc 22
                    2002512230

 ISBN 978-1-59961-891-3 (reinforced library bound edition)

All Spotlight books are reinforced library bindings
and manufactured in the United States of America.

# Chapter 1

"Knock, knock," Shaggy called from the back of the Mystery Machine.

Fred, Daphne, and Velma looked at one another.

"What did he say?" asked Velma.

"Knock, knock," Shaggy repeated.

Daphne shrugged. "Who's there?" she answered.

"Weneeda," Shaggy said.

"Weneeda who?"

"Weneeda pizza, we're starving!" Shaggy said. He and Scooby burst into laughter.

Fred shook his head and smiled.

"You walked right into that one, Daphne," he said.

"When are we going to get to Louie's?" asked Shaggy, poking his head up front.

"Reah, ren?" echoed Scooby.

"In a few minutes," Velma answered. "You two act like you haven't been to Louie's Pizza Parlor in years."

"It sure feels like it," Shaggy said.

"It's only been a few weeks, Shaggy," Daphne said.

"We're just worried he'll forget about us," Shaggy said.

"I don't think you have to worry about Louie forgetting you two," Fred said. "You're his favorite customers."

Fred steered the van into a parking space along the street. The gang jumped out and started walking down the sidewalk.

"But what if he closed the pizza parlor since our last visit?" asked Shaggy. "Then where would we go for our special pineapple, mushroom, and chocolate-chip pizzas baked on a crispy crust dripping with melted mozzarella cheese?"

Scooby licked his lips as Shaggy spoke. Just the sound of that delicious food made him hungry!

"Louie's Pizza Parlor has been in the same location for more than forty years, Shaggy," Velma said. "It's not going anywhere."

Fred stopped abruptly in front of an abandoned store.

"Uh, maybe you spoke too soon, Velma," Fred said. "Look."

He pointed to a handwritten sign taped to the window.

"'Future home of Louie's Pizza Parlor,'" Daphne read.

"Look, Scooby, another restaurant called Louie's Pizza Parlor is going to open up in town," Shaggy said. "I hope this Louie's Pizza Parlor is as good as our Louie's Pizza Parlor."

"Shaggy, it's not another Louie's Pizza Parlor," Velma said. "It's the same one. It looks to me like Louie wants to move his restaurant from across the street into this empty old building."

"Velma's right," Daphne said, examining

the poster more closely. "It says here Louie wants people to attend tonight's town council meeting to vote for the move."

"But, like, why would Louie want to move?" asked Shaggy. "He's already got the perfect pizza place."

"There's one way to find out," Fred said.

He led the gang across the street to the pizza parlor. As they approached the familiar screen door, the smell of baking pizza tickled their noses.

Scooby raised his head and took a deep breath. "Raaahhhhhhhhhh." He smiled.

"That goes double for me, Scoob," Shaggy said.

"Remember, you two, there's usually a crowd inside," Fred said. "So we may have to wait a few minutes."

"That's okay, Fred," Shaggy said. "Scooby and I will feast on the smells until our pizza's ready."

The gang stepped inside.

"Jinkies!" Velma said.

"Ruh-roh!" Scooby barked.

"Where is everybody?" Daphne wondered.

The pizza parlor was completely empty. And the mural of Italy on the far wall was splattered with paint and the words BEWARE THE CURSE OF KEE-YA.

"I don't know about you, Scoob, but I've suddenly lost my appetite," Shaggy said.

"Ree, roo," Scooby agreed.

But before they could move, a blood-curdling scream came from behind the mural.

# Chapter 2

"**W**ho's out there?" a voice called from the kitchen. Louie Farfalle, his apron stained with tomato sauce, shuffled out of the kitchen and stood behind the counter.

"Ahhhhhhh, it's my best customers," Louie said with a smile. "It's good to see some friendly faces."

"Hi, Louie," Fred said.

"Like, where is everybody?" asked Shaggy.

Daphne shot Shaggy a look. "Shaggy!" she scolded.

"No, no, it's all right," Louie said. "He's

7

right. No one's here. People come in, see those words, and walk right out again."

"Who did this?" asked Fred.

"I don't know," Louie answered glumly.

"Can't you paint over it?" asked Velma.

"I've tried, but it's some kind of fluorescent paint that keeps showing through," Louie said. "And if the words don't scare people away, the noise does."

"You mean that screaming sound we just heard?" asked Daphne.

Louie nodded slowly. "Since you were here last, a karate school opened up next door," he said. "They make all these terrible screaming sounds. I guess it's from when they chop boards in half or something. It's gotten so bad, people won't stay and eat anymore. I tried turning up the music, but then people complained about it being too loud."

"Is that why you want to move across the street?" asked Velma.

"Yes," Louie answered. "I figure over there

I won't be bothered with screams or curses."

"Like, what is the curse of Kee-Ya, anyway?" asked Shaggy.

"Kee-Ya was a famous warrior many centuries ago," came a voice from behind them. The gang turned around and saw a man wearing a karate uniform. A black belt was tied tightly around his waist. A red dragon was sewn onto the front of his jacket.

Louie took one look at the man and frowned.

"What do you want?" Louie barked.

"Pizza, Louie, what else?" the man said.

Louie grumbled and shuffled back into the kitchen.

9

"Sensei Sid," the man said, extending his hand. Fred shook it and introduced himself and the rest of the gang. "I run the karate school next door."

Sid stood up on his tiptoes to see if Louie was coming back. Then he reached over the counter and grabbed a slice of pizza.

"Legend has it that Kee-Ya hated fighting," Sensei Sid explained between bites. "But invaders threatened his town, so he invented karate and taught it to his fellow townsfolk. When the invaders showed up, Kee-Ya led his people to victory without weapons or bloodshed. All traces of the invaders, in fact, were erased from the face of the earth for all time."

"So what's his curse?" asked Velma.

"The curse is that whoever displeases the

spirit of Kee-Ya will face the same fate," Sid said, finishing off the pizza.

"Sounds creepy," Daphne said.

"Kinda like those screams," Shaggy said.

"Well, don't believe everything Louie tells you," Sid said, reaching for another slice. "We don't scream like that in Sensei Sid's Karate Kingdom. And if I have my way, no one will have to worry about any of the noise we make."

"What do you mean?" asked Fred.

"I'm going to the town council meeting tonight to convince everyone they should let me have the abandoned store across the street," Sid said. "After all, the town doesn't need a bigger pizza parlor. It needs a place where kids and adults can learn the ancient art of karate. Look at this. I've made a drawing of what it would look like."

Sensei Sid took a piece of paper from his pocket and unfolded it with one hand. As

he did, the pizza in his other hand wiggled around. Shaggy and Scooby couldn't take their eyes off the slice.

Sid admired his drawing, then slipped it back into his pocket.

"Yes, sir," he said. "There's nothing like karate to give your mind and body a good workout."

"KEEEEEEEEEE-YAAAAAAA!" someone shrieked from behind the counter. Something sailed through the air and snatched the slice of pizza from Sid's hand.

"What the —?" he gasped.

"Sidney Snallahan!" a woman yelled. "You ought to be ashamed of yourself!"

# Chapter 3

Sensei Sid spun around and faced an elderly woman in a karate stance. She wore a white apron around her waist with a notepad hanging on to it. Her hair was twisted up into a tight gray bun with two ballpoint pens sticking out.

"You've still got the moves, Mrs. F," Sid said.

"Thank you," the woman replied. "I had a good teacher."

"Thank you," Sid said.

"Jinkies, Mrs. Flibber," Velma gasped in disbelief. "That was you who just jumped

14

over the counter and grabbed Sensei Sid's pizza?"

The woman nodded as she handed the pizza to Shaggy. He licked his lips, but before he could take a bite, Scooby's tongue reached out and snatched it away.

"Louie can't stand Sid, so he sent me out to wait on him," she said. She took the pad from her apron pocket and grabbed a pen from her hair.

"Two slices of pizza," Mrs. Flibber said as she scribbled on the pad. She ripped the piece of paper off the pad and handed it to Sid. "That'll be three dollars, Sidney. And next time, don't let me catch you taking pizza without asking first."

Sid blushed a little and reached into his pocket.

"Yes, Mrs. Flibber," he said, handing her the money.

"What, no tip?" she asked.

"You want a tip?" Sid asked. "Keep your feet a little farther apart when you land." He smiled and left the pizza parlor. The screen door slammed shut and then bounced back open. Mrs. Flibber walked over to close the door. When she turned around, she noticed the gang was still staring at her.

"I know what you're thinking," she said. "How can an old woman like me move so well?"

"Well, yes," Daphne said. "We've been coming here for years and we had no idea you knew karate."

"There's a lot you don't know about me," Mrs. Flibber said.

"Like how you know Sensei Sid so well," Fred said.

"I used to baby-sit Sidney when he was a boy," Mrs. Flibber answered. "We'd watch old

kung fu movies to-
gether and act them
out. When he started
teaching karate, he
invited me to his
classes for free. I
find that karate
keeps me limber. Un-

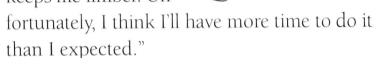

fortunately, I think I'll have more time to do it
than I expected."

"Is that because no one's coming to the
restaurant?" asked Daphne.

"That, and because Louie's going to fire
me when he moves," Mrs. Flibber said. "The
other day, I overheard him on the phone. He
said that if he moves he'll have to get rid of
the old girl."

"That's so sad," Daphne said. "I can't
imagine this place without you, Mrs. Flibber."

"I'm trying to figure out a way to get him
to stay here," Mrs. Flibber continued. "Look,

I even drew some plans for how he could fix up this place to make it more profitable and soundproof." She reached into her apron pocket and pulled out a pencil sketch of the restaurant. Then she heard the shuffling of Louie's feet and quickly stuffed it back into her apron.

"Is he gone?" Louie asked.

"He left a few minutes ago, Louie," Fred said.

"Good," Louie said. "Just the sight of him

makes my stomach curl up like a piece of rotelle."

"Like, speaking of rotelle," Shaggy said, rubbing his stomach, "how about a Scooby special and a bowl of pasta?"

A smile slowly crept across Louie's face.

"Ah, leave it to my boys to remind me of what's really important," Louie said. "Making people happy with my food. Coming right up, fellas." Louie disappeared back into the kitchen.

"Why don't you sit down and I'll get you some silverware," Mrs. Flibber said.

Just as the gang settled into a large booth, a huge gust of wind blew open the screen door.

"Rikes!" Scooby yelped.

"Like, relax, Scooby," Shaggy said. "It's just the door. I don't know what you're getting all excited about."

Another gust of wind caught the door and slammed it open and shut three times.

"Zoinks!" Shaggy cried, diving under the table.

"Oh, I've had enough of that door," Mrs. Flibber said. "Louie! I'm going down to the hardware store to get a new latch for that door before someone gets hurt!"

# Chapter 4

The gang ate their lunch as Louie tacked a tablecloth over the splattered mural.

"I see you still haven't fixed that door," a woman said as she entered the pizza parlor. The gang looked up and saw a tall woman in dark pants and a sweater standing at the counter. Some folded papers were sticking out of her rear pocket.

Louie looked at her and frowned. "Ah, never mind my door," he said. "Do you want something?"

"How about a tomato and mozzarella sandwich?" she asked.

Louie turned and shuffled back into the kitchen.

"Be a dear and make sure the basil's fresh this time, Louie!" the woman called.

"How's the bookstore, Ms. Cornflower?" Velma asked.

Brenda Cornflower turned around at the mention of her name. "Wonderful, Velma, but I haven't seen you around lately," she said.

"I've been spending more time at the library," Velma said.

"You and everyone else in this town," Brenda muttered. "Here, look at this." She squeezed herself into the booth next to Fred. "Do you mind if I sit down? I've been dying to show someone this all morning."

She took the papers from her pocket. She unfolded them on the table, sliding Shaggy's and Scooby's plates to one side to make room.

"What do you think of this?" Brenda asked.

"What is it?" asked Daphne.

"It looks like a floor plan," Velma said. "Let me guess. It's for the empty store across the street."

"Why, however did you know that, Velma?" Brenda asked.

"It seems you're not the only person interested in it," Fred answered.

"I know, but I'm the only person who's really got a chance of getting the town council's approval," Brenda said. "After all, who'd vote for a pizza place or a karate school if

they could vote for something that will give this town some culture and sophistication?"

"Like, right now I'd settle for my pizza and spaghetti," Shaggy whispered to Scooby. They reached over for their plates.

"Careful, Shaggy dear," Brenda said. "You wouldn't want to get sauce all over my drawings, would you?"

"No, just all over my mouth," Shaggy said.

Louie shuffled out of the kitchen carrying a plate with a sandwich on it.

"Brenda, stop bothering my customers," Louie said. "And stop putting ideas into their heads. No one's going to vote for a bookstore or a karate school. The mayor's already told me they plan to vote for me. They just need the town council's vote to make it official. And they're not going to change their minds."

Brenda folded up her plans and smiled.

"But they'll have to change their minds, Louie," Brenda said. "Once you change yours and decide you don't want to move, that is."

"Now why would I do that?" asked Louie.

Brenda shrugged and walked toward the door.

"What about your sandwich?" Louie called.

"Oh, I'll just take it to go," Brenda said. She walked back to the table and picked up the plate. "See you later, Louie." She left the restaurant, plate in hand.

"Hey! That's my plate!" Louie called. "Ahhhhhh, never mind. Sometimes I wish I'd never even opened this restaurant."

Shaggy and Scooby stopped eating and stared at Louie.

"Like, don't ever say that, Louie," Shaggy said.

"I'm sorry, boys," Louie said. "Didn't mean to upset you. Maybe when you're done, you can help drum up some business. It'd be nice to have a full restaurant again."

"Like, leave it to me and Scooby!" Shaggy said.

# Chapter 5

Later that afternoon, Louie stood behind the counter of his empty restaurant, twirling pizza dough. Fred, Daphne, and Velma were helping fold menus and napkins.

"Thanks for helping out, kids," Louie said. "It's not like Mrs. Flibber to be gone for so long."

"It's our pleasure, Louie," Daphne said.

Velma suddenly looked up from what she was doing. "Do you hear that?" she asked.

Everyone heard a faint pounding sound in the distance.

The pounding slowly got louder.

"It sounds like . . . like a marching band," Fred said.

Suddenly, the screen door flew open. In marched Shaggy and Scooby leading a crowd of people. Scooby was beating a bass drum that was almost as big as he was. The people found seats at the empty tables.

"Here you go, Louie," Shaggy said. "One full restaurant, as ordered."

Louie smiled. "Thanks, kids, but when I

28

asked you to drum up business, I didn't ex-
pect you to take me literally."

"Jinkies, Shaggy, how did you and Scooby
do it?" Velma asked.

"Like, it was nothing," Shaggy said.
"Scooby and I borrowed the drum from the
music store around the corner. We marched
around the town. Scooby beat the drum and
I shouted out the name of the restaurant."

"Rand ree rizza," Scooby said.

Louie's eyes nearly popped out of his head. "Free pizza?" he repeated.

"Shaggy, how could you?" Daphne scolded. "Louie can't afford to feed everyone for free."

"Ahhhhhh, it's okay, Daphne," Louie said. "One bite of a free slice of pizza and they'll want to order a whole pie."

"We'll help you serve until Mrs. Flibber gets back," Daphne said.

"And Scooby and I will help you cook," Shaggy said.

But before anyone could move, a loud, piercing shriek filled the pizza parlor.

"KEEEEEEEE-YA!"

The screen door flew open again. Someone or some*thing* flipped through the air and landed in front of the pizza counter.

"Zoinks!" Shaggy cried.

The creature was dressed in a black karate uniform, black boots, black gloves, and a black mask that covered its entire head. Glowing red eyes were the only features on its face.

"I am the curse of Kee-Ya!" the creature hissed. It reached over the counter and grabbed a freshly baked pizza. Kee-Ya placed the metal pizza pan on the table and spun it around. Then, with lightning-fast hands, the karate creature chopped at the spinning pizza.

"KEEEEE-YA-YA-YA-YA-YA-YA-YA!" it cried.

When the pizza stopped spinning, it was sliced into tiny wedges.

"This pizza place must not move," the karate creature warned. "For if it does, the curse of Kee-Ya will remain with it and whoever eats here, forever!"

The karate creature sprang into a karate

pose and then slowly brought its hands together. It rubbed its palms quickly and then clapped them together. "KEEEEEE-YA!"

The karate creature raised a hand and smashed it down on one of the tables. The table cracked and split in two. The karate creature laughed as it leaped into the air and sprang out the door. The customers quickly followed.

"Wait!" Louie cried. "Don't go! It was just a little karate show. A commercial for the karate school next door. Hold on! Free pizza and free ravioli for everyone!"

But it was too late. Everyone streamed toward the door. The few customers who stayed behind told Louie to listen to the karate creature and forget about moving.

"Listen, Louie, I'll do you a favor and urge the town council to vote against you tonight," one customer said on his way out. "You can thank me tomorrow."

Louie looked around his empty restaurant. "Ahhhhhh, maybe they're right," Louie said. "I can't compete with that creepy karate thing running around here. Look what it did to my table."

"You take care of your restaurant, Louie," Fred said. "And let us take care of the karate creature."

# Chapter 6

"So where do we start?" asked Daphne.

"How about with the free pizza and ravioli?" asked Shaggy. "Scooby and I hate to do detective work on an empty stomach."

"You two hate to do detective work, period," Velma said. "But if you want Louie's Pizza Parlor to stay open, you'll help us solve this mystery."

Louie started shuffling back toward the kitchen.

"Where are you going, Louie?" asked Fred.

"To my office," Louie said. "I want to write

a letter to the town council withdrawing my request. Just in case."

The gang heard the office door click shut.

"If we're going to solve this mystery before the meeting tonight, we have to act fast," Fred said. "I say we split up now."

"Good idea, Fred," Velma said. "Shaggy, Scooby, and I will look around in here."

"Fred, you and I can check out the street," Daphne suggested. "Maybe the karate creature left some clues when it came in or left."

Fred nodded. "Let's meet back here as soon as possible. Good luck, everyone."

Fred and Daphne walked outside, carefully closing the screen door behind them.

"Jinkies, what a mess," Velma said.

"Like, that karate creature must have really sharp hands to chop all this stuff up," Shaggy said.

"You don't need sharp hands, Shaggy, just quick ones," Velma said. "Karate is one of the most ancient of the martial arts. But it's really a system of defense, so it's not meant to be used to scare people. Anyway, let's look around."

Velma walked over to the door and looked up in the air. "The karate creature flipped through the air from here and landed over by the counter," she said. "Then it stepped over to the table to cut up the pizza. Then it went over there and chopped that table in half. Then it leaped through the air to leave. Shaggy, you and Scooby look around the counter area. I'll look around the tables."

Shaggy and Scooby stood by the counter. Scooby sniffed around the floor. Shaggy went behind the counter to look around. Scooby sniffed higher and Shaggy searched lower. Their noses met in the middle.

"Hey, Scooby," Shaggy whispered. "Are you thinking what I'm thinking?"

Scooby smiled and wagged his tail. "Rou ret!" he barked.

"No funny business, you two," Velma called. "We're looking for clues."

"So are we, Velma," Shaggy called back.

"I found something!" Velma called. She reached down near the broken table and picked up a torn piece of paper with some pencil lines drawn on it.

"Take a look at this, fellas," Velma called. She walked over to the counter and looked around. There was no sign of Shaggy and Scooby.

"Shaggy? Scooby?" she called.

Shaggy and Scooby suddenly popped up from behind the counter.

"Would you like mushrooms or anchovies on that?" Shaggy said.

"I thought I told you two not to fool around," Velma said.

"Like, we were looking for clues, Velma, honest," Shaggy said.

"I'm going to find Fred and Daphne and show them what I found," Velma said. She headed outside, leaving Shaggy and Scooby behind the counter.

"Ready, pal?" asked Shaggy.

"Ready!" Scooby replied.

They each picked up a ball of dough and tossed it into the air to make pizzas. The dough balls plopped back onto the counter in an enormous cloud of flour.

"I guess we need some help with our technique," Shaggy coughed. As he and Scooby fanned the flour away, they heard someone coming from the kitchen.

"Sorry, Louie, but we can explain," Shaggy said.

But before he could say anything else,

Shaggy and Scooby heard a familiar and unsettling sound.

"KEEEEEEE-YA!"

# Chapter 7

As the cloud of flour cleared, Shaggy and Scooby stood face-to-mask with the karate creature.

"Rikes!" Scooby cried.

"Let's go, Scoob!" Shaggy yelled.

Shaggy and Scooby threw open the door and ran out onto the sidewalk.

"Help! It's after us!" Shaggy cried.

Fred and Daphne ran to their friends from one direction and Velma ran over from the other.

"Take it easy, Shaggy," Daphne said. "You're

saying the karate creature was just back in the restaurant?"

"Rou ret," Scooby said. He assumed a karate pose and chopped at the air with his paw. "Ree-ya! Ree-ya! Ree-ya!"

"Okay, Scoob, we get the picture," Fred said.

Shaggy and Scooby turned to run the other way and smacked right into Mrs. Flibber. She staggered back and dropped the bag from the hardware store.

"Oh my stars," she said.

"Sorry, Mrs. Flibber," Shaggy said. "But the karate creature was after us."

"What karate creature?" asked Mrs. Flibber.

"Kee-Ya," Fred and Daphne said. Fred picked up the bag and handed it to her. "A little while ago, the spirit of Kee-Ya came to the restaurant and made quite a scene."

"And quite a mess," Daphne added. "We've been looking for clues to help us figure out this mystery."

"I see," Mrs. Flibber said. "I'd better go check on Louie and get the door fixed. Good luck."

Mrs. Flibber disappeared into the pizza parlor.

"I wonder why she didn't seem scared," Fred said.

"Maybe because she didn't just come face-to-face with Creepy Karate Hands," Shaggy said.

"Speaking of the karate creature," Velma

said, "take a look at what I found inside the pizza place."

She showed Fred and Daphne the drawing.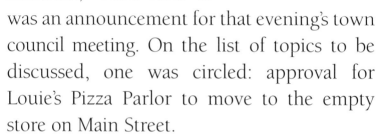

"Here's what Daphne and I found out here on the sidewalk," Fred said. It was an announcement for that evening's town council meeting. On the list of topics to be discussed, one was circled: approval for Louie's Pizza Parlor to move to the empty store on Main Street.

"These are good clues, but there's still something I don't understand," Daphne said. "We found some people who said they saw the karate creature run out of the pizza place and go down the street that way. How could it have gotten back to the pizza place so quickly?"

"Maybe the karate creature used the back

door," Velma said. "When I came out here to look for you guys, I saw a bunch of students go into the karate school next door. I went to have a look and found a narrow alley on the far side of the building. I have a hunch the alley leads back behind the buildings."

"I'll bet there's one down the other way, too," Fred said.

"And I'll bet that's how the karate creature could leave through the front door and come back through the back door so quickly," Daphne said.

"Let's go check it out," Velma said.

The gang walked down the street. Two stores down, just past Brenda Cornflower's bookstore, the gang found another alley. They walked down the alley to the rear of the buildings. Then they walked back up to the pizza parlor's back door. Fred, Daphne, and Velma looked around. Scooby started sniffing all over.

"Okay, so this is the back door," Shaggy said. "What's the big deal?"

"Well, Shaggy, I guess there is no big deal after all," Fred said. "Nothing around here but empty flour bags and broken-down boxes."

"Rand rooks," Scooby said.

"Books? What books?" asked Velma.

Scooby pointed to a book sticking out from under the pile of flour bags.

Daphne reached down and picked up the book. She blew off a thin coating of flour.

"This book looks like it's brand-new," Daphne said.

"It's a brand-new how-to," Velma said.

"How to do what?" asked Fred.

Daphne looked up. "Karate," she said.

"You know what this means, gang," Fred said. "It's time to set a trap."

# Chapter 8

"We don't have much time, Fred," Daphne said. "The town council's going to meet soon."

"I know," Fred answered. "So we have to get the karate creature to come back to Louie's one more time."

"Then let's make it obvious that Louie's still going ahead with his plan to move," Velma suggested. "We can put a big sign in the window."

"That's a good start, Velma," Fred said. "But we'll have to go even further. And for that, we're going to need your help, Scooby."

"Ro ray," Scooby said, shaking his head.

"Scooby, will you help us for a super pineapple, mushroom, chocolate-chip pizza?" asked Daphne.

Scooby licked his lips.

"Remember the karate creature, Scoob," Shaggy whispered.

"Ruh-uh," Scooby said, coming back to his senses.

"How about a super pineapple, mushroom, and chocolate-chip pizza later and a Scooby Snack right now?" asked Daphne.

"Rokay!" Scooby barked.

Daphne tossed a Scooby Snack into the air and Scooby gobbled it down. He licked his lips with his big pink tongue.

"So here's what we'll do," Fred said. "Daphne, you and Velma go inside and make the new sign for the window. Be sure to mention the arrival of Chef Scoobino from Italy to help with the grand opening."

"Who's Chef Scoobino?" Shaggy asked.

"You're looking at him," Fred said. "Scooby, you'll stand behind the counter, pretending to be Chef Scoobino."

"Rehind ruh rounter?" asked Scooby. "Roh, roy!"

"I said *pretending* to be a chef," Fred said, smiling. "Shaggy, you and I will hide behind the tablecloth that Louie hung on the wall. When the karate creature shows up, Scooby, you distract it. Shaggy and I will jump out and capture it in the tablecloth. Okay?"

"Roger," Scooby said.

"I'll go tell Louie the plan," Fred said. "Shaggy, help Scooby get ready." Fred, Velma, and Daphne went inside to prepare.

"Let's go, pal," Shaggy said. He and

Scooby walked into the kitchen. Shaggy found another apron and tied it around Scooby's middle. Shaggy reached into a bowl of cooked spaghetti and pulled out some strands. He twirled them into a long mustache and stuck them just below Scooby's nose. On top of a tall rack of pans Shaggy spied a chef's hat. He reached up and grabbed the hat, placing it carefully on Scooby's head.

"Ready, fellas?" Fred called from the front of the restaurant.

"Coming, Fred," Shaggy called back. Shaggy and Scooby walked out front. "Presenting Chef Scoobino. Good luck, pal."

Scooby stood behind the counter, and

Shaggy hid with Fred behind the hanging tablecloth. Velma and Daphne hung a sign in the window that announced the arrival of Chef Scoobino. Then they ran and hid in the back.

Scooby started trying to make another pizza. He patted out a ball of dough. He picked it up in his paws and started stretching it. Then he spun it up into the air and watched it fall right on top of his head.

"Ree-hee-hee-hee-hee-hee-hee-heeee," he giggled.

But just then, a piercing sound sent chills up Scooby's spine.

"KEEEEEE-YA!"

Then there was a crash outside the door. A moment later, Scooby heard someone struggle with the screen door. As the door slowly creaked open, Scooby pulled the pizza dough away from his eyes. The karate creature limped into the restaurant and looked around. It spied Scooby and hissed.

"Rikes!" Scooby cried, diving behind the counter.

"The curse of Kee-Ya is with you forever, Chef Scoobino!" the karate creature roared. It stepped toward the counter and raised its black-gloved hand. Just as it was about to karate-chop the counter, the creature heard a noise behind it and spun around.

"No one can sneak up on the curse of Kee-Ya!" it hissed at Shaggy and Fred. And before they knew what had happened, the karate creature's lightning-fast hands had wrapped them up in the tablecloth.

The creature turned back to the counter, but Scooby was gone.

"Rover rere!" Scooby called.

The creature spun around again and saw Scooby standing on a table. The karate creature leaped into the air and landed on the other end of the table. Scooby flew into the air over the karate creature and landed behind the counter again.

Just as the karate creature leaped over the counter, Scooby stood up, his chef's hat over his eyes. The creature's feet got caught in the hat and fell to the ground. Scooby jumped onto the counter to get away. And as he did, he knocked an entire bag of flour right onto the karate creature.

The karate creature struggled to get up, but was trapped beneath a pile of pizza flour.

# Chapter 9

ouie ran out from the back with Velma and Daphne. Velma unwrapped Fred and Shaggy. Daphne made sure Scooby was all right. Then Fred and Louie pulled the karate creature to its feet. Its black costume was now white, giving it a ghostly appearance.

"Well, Louie, are you ready to see who's been behind all this?" asked Fred.

Louie nodded and reached over. He grabbed the karate creature's mask and yanked it off.

"Ahhhhhh, Brenda Cornflower!" Louie

exclaimed. "You're guilty of trying to ruin me?"

"Just as we suspected," Velma said.

"You knew this, Velma?" asked Louie. "How could you know?"

"It wasn't easy, Louie," Daphne said. "At least not at first. There were a lot of people we initially suspected."

"Like Sensei Sid, Brenda, and even Mrs. Flibber," Fred said. "They all had reasons for not wanting you to move the pizza parlor."

"And they all showed us something that matched our first clue," Velma said. "Part of a floor plan for the new space. Or in Mrs. Flibber's case, for this old space."

"So that first clue just confirmed who our suspects were," Fred said. "But the next clue helped us narrow it down a bit."

"Outside we found a notice for the town council meeting," Daphne said. "And the agenda item about the pizza place and the empty building was circled. That told us the karate creature was particularly interested in that part of the meeting."

"Just like Sid and Brenda," Fred said. "Both of them made no secret about planning to convince the town council to vote against you."

"But it was the final clue that put it all together," Velma said. "We realized that the karate creature used the back door when it returned to scare Shaggy and Scooby. So we checked out the rear of the pizza parlor and found this."

Velma held up the book that Scooby had found.

"'*Karate for Kicks: From Basics to Black Belt in Ten Easy Lessons*,'" read Louie. "So, it's a karate book."

"It's a brand-new karate book," Daphne

said. "Something you could easily get in a bookstore."

"And something that a karate expert, like Sid or Mrs. Flibber, wouldn't need," Fred said.

"Brenda, why go through all this trouble?" asked Louie.

"Because I needed to expand my bookstore quickly," Brenda said. "Ever since the town remodeled the library, people stopped coming to my store. They had everything over there. Everything except the things I was going to put into my new store, like a coffee shop, and an ice-cream parlor, and even a pizza oven. I had big plans for that space. And I would've gotten away with it, too. But then those kids and their nosy dog got involved."

Mrs. Flibber came in with two policemen. "I heard such a commotion that I called the police," she said. "Is everything all right?"

"It is, thanks to the kids," Louie said.

Each of the policemen took one of Brenda's

arms and led her away. "I understand why Sid and Brenda wouldn't want me to move, but why you, Mrs. Flibber?" Louie asked.

"Because, Louie, I overheard you saying that once you moved you'd have to get rid of the old girl," Mrs. Flibber said. "Sound familiar?"

Louie thought for a moment and then started laughing.

"I was talking about the old pizza oven, not you, Mrs. Flibber," Louie said. "Of course I'd need you in the new place. More than ever. Who could run the dining room better than you?"

Mrs. Flibber blushed. "Well, maybe I did overreact a bit," she said.

"Hey, Louie, congratulations!" Sensei Sid called through the screen door. "The town council just met. They gave you the store. And they're going to let me knock down the wall between us and expand my school. So we're both winners."

"That's wonderful, Louie," Daphne said.

"Thank you, Daphne," Louie said. "But it

never would have happened if it wasn't for Scooby. He's a true hero. How can I thank him?"

"Like, how about that free pizza and ravioli you mentioned earlier today?" asked Shaggy.

"I have an even better idea," Louie said. "I'll be right back."

Louie disappeared into the kitchen and returned a moment later carrying a plate. On it sat an enormous sandwich.

"What better way to thank a hero than with a hero?" Louie announced. "Presenting

Louie's Pizza Parlor's newest creation, the Scooby-Doo Super-duper Hero's Hero Sandwich!"

Scooby eyed the huge sandwich and licked his lips. He opened his mouth and took a gigantic bite.

"Rbflbfy-dbfffbbllby-dooooo!"